This Walker book belongs to:

_____

_____

_____

For
RALPH
and the
NATURAL
THEATRE CO.

First published 1993 by Walker Books Ltd, 87 Vauxhall Walk, London SE11 5HJ

This edition published 2010

2 4 6 8 10 9 7 5 3

© 1993 Penny Dale

The right of Penny Dale to be identified as author/illustrator of this work
has been asserted by her in accordance with the Copyright, Designs and Patents Act 1988

This book has been typeset in Bookman

Printed in China

British Library Cataloguing in Publication Data:
a catalogue record for this book is available from the British Library

ISBN 978-1-4063-2884-4

www.walker.co.uk

TEN OUT OF BED

PENNY DALE

WALKER BOOKS
AND SUBSIDIARIES

LONDON • BOSTON • SYDNEY • AUCKLAND

There were ten out of bed...

and the little one said, "Let's play!"

So they all played trains
until Hedgehog fell asleep.

There were nine out of bed
and the little one said,
"Let's play!"

And Ted said,
"Let's play SEASIDES!"

So nine played seasides
until Ted fell asleep.

There were eight out of bed
and the little one said,
"Let's play!"

And Rabbit said,
"Let's play THEATRES!"

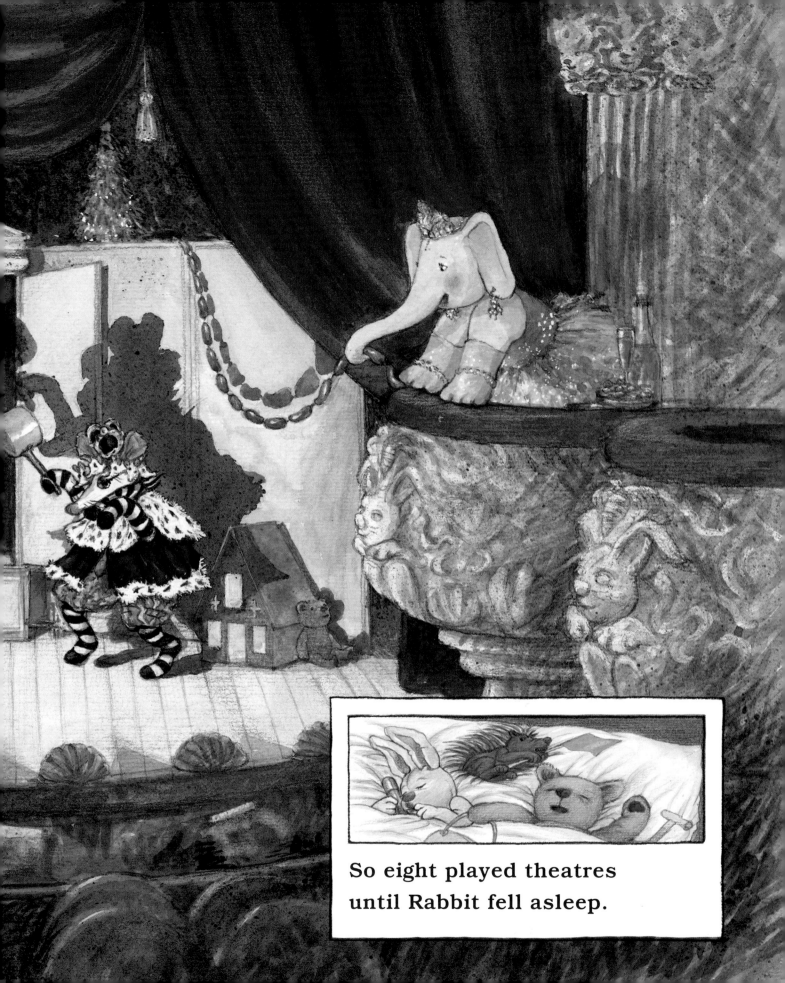

So eight played theatres
until Rabbit fell asleep.

So seven played pirates
until Bear fell asleep.

There were six out of bed
and the little one said,
"Let's play!"

And Sheep said,
"Let's play DANCING!"

So six played dancing
until Sheep fell asleep.

There were five out of bed
and the little one said,
"Let's play!"

And Croc said,
"Let's play GHOSTS!"

So five played ghosts
until Croc fell asleep.

So four played flying
until Nellie fell asleep.

There were three out of bed
and the little one said,
"Let's play!"

And Zebra said,
"Let's play CAMPING!"

So three played camping
until Zebra fell asleep.

There were two out of bed
and the little one said,
"Let's play!"

And Mouse said,
"Let's play MONSTERS!"

So two played monsters
until Mouse fell asleep.

There was one out of bed and the little one said,

"I'm sleepy now!"

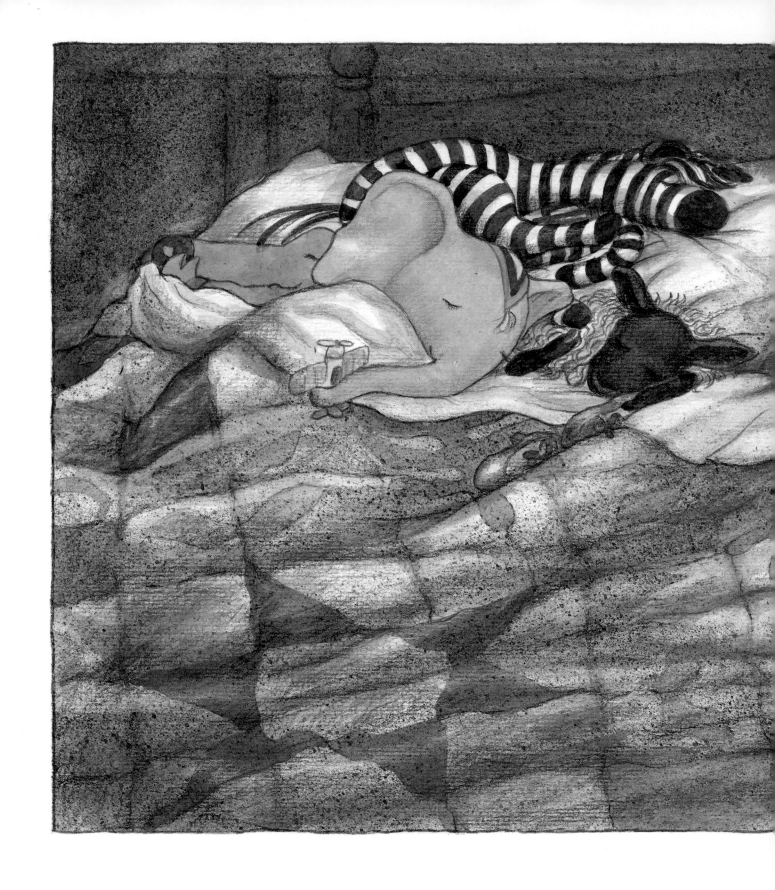

So he slipped under the covers next to Ted.

Good night, sweet dreams, ten in the bed.

Books by Penny Dale

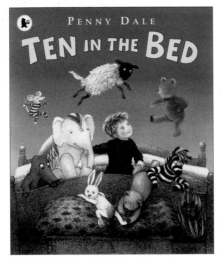

ISBN 978-1-4063-0035-2

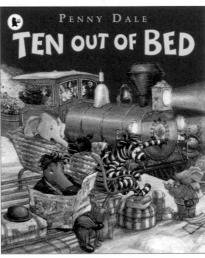

ISBN 978-1-4063-2884-4

ISBN 978-1-4063-2885-1

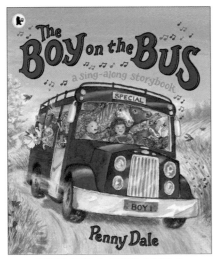

ISBN 978-1-4063-1233-1

ISBN 978-1-84428-465-8

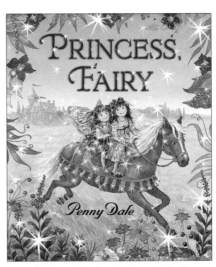

ISBN 978-1-4063-1574-5

Available from all good bookstores

www.walker.co.uk